Oriental Cats

by Gail Lewis

Consulting Editor: Gail Saunders-Smith, PhD

Consultant: Jennifer Zablotny, DVM
Member, American Veterinary Medical Association

Mankato, Minnesota

Pebble Books are published by Capstone Press,
151 Good Counsel Drive, P.O. Box 669, Mankato, Minnesota 56002.
www.capstonepress.com

Copyright © 2009 by Capstone Press, a Capstone Publishers company.
All rights reserved.
No part of this publication may be reproduced in whole or in part,
or stored in a retrieval system, or transmitted in any form or by any means,
electronic, mechanical, photocopying, recording, or otherwise,
without written permission of the publisher.
For information regarding permission, write to Capstone Press,
151 Good Counsel Drive, P.O. Box 669, Dept. R, Mankato, Minnesota 56002.
Printed in the United States of America

1 2 3 4 5 6 13 12 11 10 09 08

Library of Congress Cataloging-in-Publication Data
Lewis, Gail, 1970–
    Oriental cats / by Gail Lewis.
    p. cm. — (Pebble Books. Cats)
    Includes bibliographical references and index.
    Summary: "Simple text and photographs present an introduction to the Oriental breed, its growth from kitten to adult, and pet care information" — Provided by publisher.
    ISBN-13: 978-1-4296-1715-4 (hardcover)
    ISBN-10: 1-4296-1715-2 (hardcover)
    1. Oriental shorthair cat — Juvenile literature. I. Title.
SF449.O73L49 2009
636.8'2 — dc22   2007051273

Note to Parents and Teachers

The Cats set supports national science standards related to life science. This book describes and illustrates Oriental cats. The images support early readers in understanding the text. The repetition of words and phrases helps early readers learn new words. This book also introduces early readers to subject-specific vocabulary words, which are defined in the Glossary section. Early readers may need assistance to read some words and to use the Table of Contents, Glossary, Read More, Internet Sites, and Index sections of the book.

Table of Contents

Colorful Cats 5
From Kitten to Adult 11
Caring for Orientals 17

Glossary. 22
Read More 23
Internet Sites. 23
Index 24

Colorful Cats

Orientals are
a very colorful
kind of cat.

Orientals have any
of 300 different colors
and patterns of fur.

Orientals have soft fur.
Their fur can be
long or short.

From Kitten to Adult

Newborn Orientals have short, thin fur. They snuggle together to stay warm.

Orientals have faces
that look like triangles.
Their ears are big
like kites.

Orientals grow up
to be thin but strong.
Oriental cats have
tails that are
long and thin.

Caring for Orientals

Orientals are active and curious cats. They need to exercise and play every day.

Orientals need food and water every day.

Orientals like to be with their owners. An Oriental cat is a good friend.

Glossary

active — being able to exercise, play, and move around

curious — eager to explore and learn about new things

exercise — physical activity done in order to stay healthy and fit

owner — a person who has something; pets need owners who care for them.

pattern — a repeating order of colors and shapes

Read More

Barnes, Julia. *Pet Cats.* Pet Pals. Milwaukee: Gareth Stevens, 2007.

Shores, Erika L. *Caring for Your Cat.* Positively Pets. Mankato, Minn.: Capstone Press, 2007.

Internet Sites

FactHound offers a safe, fun way to find Internet sites related to this book. All of the sites on FactHound have been researched by our staff.

Here's how:

1. Visit *www.facthound.com*
2. Choose your grade level.
3. Type in this book ID **1429617152** for age-appropriate sites. You may also browse subjects by clicking on letters, or by clicking on pictures and words.
4. Click on the **Fetch It** button.

FactHound will fetch the best sites for you!

Index

active, 17
colors, 5, 7
curious, 17
ears, 13
exercise, 17
faces, 13
food, 19
fur, 7, 9, 11

kittens, 11
owners, 21
patterns, 7
playing, 17
size, 15
strong, 15
tails, 15
water, 19

Word Count: 107
Grade: 1
Early-Intervention Level: 12

Editorial Credits
Lori Shores, editor; Renée T. Doyle, set designer; Danielle Ceminsky, book designer; Wanda Winch, photo researcher

Photo Credits
Alamy/tbkmedia.de, 6
Ardea/Jean Michel Labat, 8
Fiona Green, 4, 10, 16, 18, 20
fotolia/Katerina Cherkashina, 1, 12, 22, cover
Getty Images Inc./Dorling Kindersley/Marc Henrie, 14

SAYVILLE LIBRARY
11 COLLINS AVE.
SAYVILLE, NY 11782

DEC - 5 2008

**DISCARDED BY
SAYVILLE LIBRARY**